My O Book

by Jane Belk Moncure

illillustrated by Vera Gohman

THE CHILD'S WORLD

ELGIN, ILLINOIS 60120

Library of Congress Cataloging in Publication Data

Moncure, Jane Belk.
  My "o" book.

  (My first steps to reading)
  Rev. ed. of: My "o" sound box. © 1984.
  Summary: Little "o" fills his box with otters, an
octopus, an ostrich, and other things beginning with the
short letter "o."
  1. Children's stories, American.   [1. Alphabet]
I. Gohman, Vera Kennedy, 1922-   ill.   II. Moncure,
Jane Belk.   My "o" sound box.   III. Title.   IV. Series:
Moncure, Jane Belk.   My first steps to reading.
PZ7.M739Myo   1984b   [E]   84-17538
ISBN 0-89565-275-7

Distributed by Childrens Press, 1224 West Van Buren Street,
Chicago, Illinois 60607.

My "o" Book

(This book uses only the short "o" sound in the story line. Words beginning with the long "o" sound are included at the end of the book.)

Little  had a box.

He said, "I will fill my box."

Little ⬤ hopped away,

hop, hop, hop.

He found

otters

in a pond.

He put the

otters

into his box.

Little

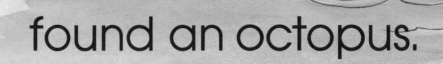

found an octopus.

Guess where he put
the octopus?

But the otters did
not like the octopus.

The otters hopped out
of the box,

hop, hop, hop.

Little  put a top on the box, so the octopus could not get out.

Then he put the otters on top
of the box.

Away he went, hop, hop, hop.

Then Little found an ostrich.

He hopped on
the ostrich.

"Hop,"
he said.

But the ostrich would not hop.

So Little O put the ostrich on top of the box.

19

Now the box was heavy.

Little  found an

O

ox.

"You are just what I need
for my box," he said.

Away they went,
hop,
hop,

all the way home.

Little **O** took his things out of his box.

octopus

ox

ostrich

otters

What funny things he had!

More words with Little .

October

S	M	T	W	T	F	S
		1	2	3	4	5	6
7	8	9	10	11	12	13
14	15	16	17	18	19	20
21	22	23	24	25	26	27
28	29	30	31			

olives

operator

ocelot

omnibus

Little  has another sound in some words.

He says his name.
Listen for Little 's name.

overalls

okra

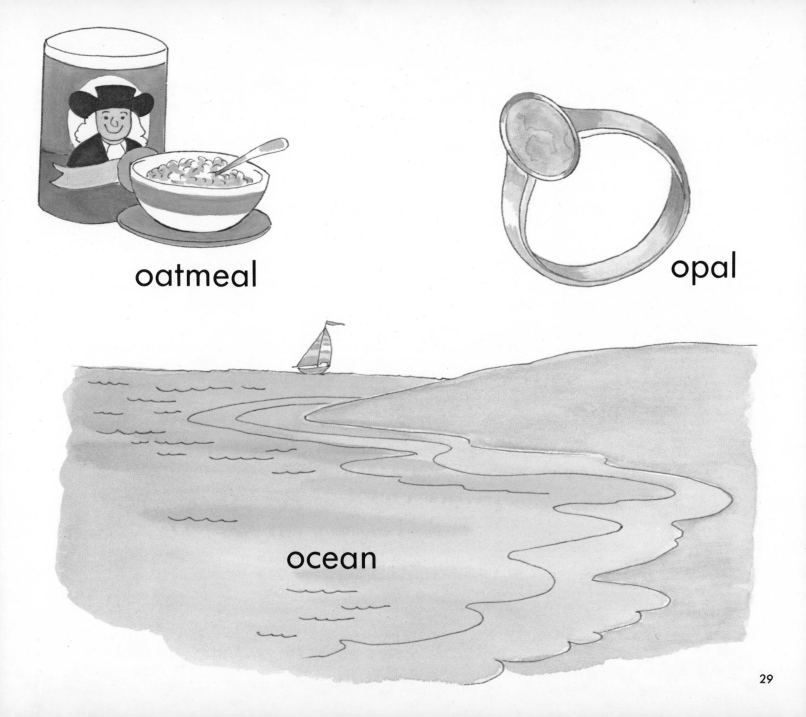

oatmeal

opal

ocean

29